# When We Were Dragons

By

Zeni Workman

# Dedication

To Nickey and Will! Here's the story we created together!

When We Were Dragons Language Key (2)

1. The Knowing One/Na Mananda/Language Batak Toba

2. Beautiful World/Mundu Ederra/Language Basque

3. Ruby City/Vita Rubia/Language Corsican

4. Golden Lake/Ora Lago/Language Esperanto

5. Young One/Bata/Language Filipino

6. Silver Mountains/Gunong Perak/Language Acehnese

7. Jade trees/Jade Arbores de Cortiza/ Language Latin

8. Ember Stone/ Tuunich Ember/Language Yucatec Maya

9. "My Name" Zenfire/ Zennure/Language Kanuri

10. The Caring One/Zaintzea/ Language Basque

11. Delicious Food/ Cibo Delizioso/ Language Italian

12. Cattle/ Bawng/ Language Mizo

13. Meat Stew/Ragout de Viande/ Language French

14. Four/ Cuatro/ Language Spanish

15. Strong/ Fuerte/ Language Spanish

16. Crystal Bark Tree/Arbores de Cortiza de Cristal/Language Galician

17. Evil Incarnate/Kyha/Language Yakut

18. Unicorn/Dwec/Language Acholi

19.     Five/Cinco/Language Spanish

20.     No Tail Lizard/ Alaa Wutte Wutte/ Language

Fulani

21.     Two Moons/Uwer Uhar/Language/Tiv

22.     Loyal One/Lelle/Language Sicilian

23.     Oldest Brother/ Frare Mia Ancian/Language

Occittan

24.     First One/Eerste Een/Language Africaans

25.     Mother of Nature/I Tinaq/Language Fijian

26.     Spirit Breath/ Souffle/Language French

27.     Life Spirit/Eletzellem/Language Hungarian

28.     Telekinesis Transportation/Transporto Teleinine/Language Italian

29.     Dear Friend/ Cher Ami/Language French

30.     Home Galaxy/Galeksi Rumah/ Language

Balinese

# Table of Contents

# Chapter 1

In a space before time was young, there was infinite beauty, happiness, and loyalty to our creator, called *The Knowing*, Na Mananda.[1]

You can see it if you close your eyes and open your heart.

Let us fly like we used to. Hear all, and know all that there was and ever will be. Let us go now to the very first land, the place where all is touched by Knowing. The place of our birth: *Mundu Ederra.*[2]

**When we were dragons!**

We now fly back through time,

before there were people,

before Na Mananda[1] created the dinosaurs,

back before the stars were young.

To the land where Na Mananda[1] was born.

Can you see it? It is like an ever-glowing ember, a kaleidoscope of brilliant colors, a glowing orb. It is the largest planet in the First Galaxy, named *Mundu Ederra.*[2]

But wait, we cannot land until we transform into our former glory: our dragon selves.

Now, just fly through the Pearl Arches. The transformation is taking place.

Our hands and feet are now five-toed claws.

Our back is ridged with spikes, like The  Silver Mountains, *Gunong Perak.*[3]

We now have a long, spiked tail.

We have pointed ears and a long snout.

Our mouth is wide and full of pointed teeth.

Oh my, our skin is now scales. But each of us has different colors of scales.

Mine is like a multicolored pearl of fire.

Yours is glowing golden green.

It is time to fly to our homeland: *Vita Rubia,3.*

Who will we see?

Who will still be there?

Will we see Na Mananda?[2]

# CHAPTER 2
# WHAT TIME ARE WE IN

Through the Kaleidoscope Aglow atmosphere, down through the Misty Pearl clouds, we can see the Golden Lakes, Ora Lago, (4) and the Silver Mountains, Gunong Perak! (6) At last, we land beside the Jade-Leave Trees, Yade Yadi, (7) and feel the cotton-soft turquoise grass on our feet!

Let's explore.

Through the Pearl clouds, the nearest Young Star's illuminating rays warmed my scales. It creates a crystalline light that illuminates Mundu Ederra (2) like shining light through a crystal glass, creating hues of rainbows throughout the sky. When it shines in The Jade Trees, Yade Yadi, (7) it leaves a green shadow on the red dirt and turquoise grass!

Do you see that in the sky? It's an Orange Neon Fish! It's like it's swimming—but in the air!

It's time to get a drink from the Ora Lago. (4) The golden sheen is a mirror reflection. For the first time in a long time, I can see my true self!

I am Zennure. (9)

"Come over here and see what you look like, Bata!" (5) I invite.

"I look so different, but wonderful!" you exclaimed. "This world is so fantastic!"

I can see the amazement in your eyes.

"You have to part the golden water to drink from the Ora Lago," (4) I told Bata. (5)

I taste the purple water underneath the golden sheen. It tastes like the grapes on Earth! But I feel something happening! I feel my mind growing more intelligent. Suddenly, I see in my mind all that was and all that ever will be!

I feel the entire universe is now told to me.

I see the entire universe being created—worlds, galaxies, billions of them! Each of them has their own inhabited planets. I can see the creation of planets, animals, the sea and its creatures, of every inhabited world in every different galaxy! Knowledge must be in the water!

"How do you feel after you've drunk the water, Bata?" (5) I'm curious.

"I'm getting hungry. How about you?" Bata (5) inquires.

"Does the water make you feel any different?" I ask.

"Not sure, but I do want to eat," Bata remarks.

I wonder why Bata (5) isn't affected?

"Let's go find something to eat! Remember that we can fly! Let's take flight and find Vita Rubia (3) to the east. There we will search for my family, and we will have a feast!" I endeavor.

# EXCITEMENT ANTICIPATION

The closer we get to Vita Rubia (3), the more anxious and excited I feel. Who will be there? Will I see my family? Has time stood still?

At last we have Vita Rubia (3) in our sight!

"Do you see it, Bata (5)?" I inquired.

"Oh my goodness! Its roofs are shining like beautiful rubies!" Bata (5) excitedly remarks.

"All the roofs are made of rubies and the walls are all white but shine like the inside of a sea shell!" Bata (5) remarks astoundedly.

"Can you smell all the different flowers? They're like the ones that are on Earth, except these can get up and move around! They're kept like pets and trained like dogs!" I told Bata (5).

As we landed just outside of the gates, I can hear the busy city sounds.

"Let's stick together because no one knows you," I cautioned.

# CHAPTER 3
# EVERYTHING OLD IS NEW



Passing through the gates, we can smell the different meals cooking! Lined along the inside walls are street vendors selling various wares like Tuunich Ember (Ember stone) (8) used to eat! So we can breathe fire! Enrichment scale scrub, Pumice Stone, used to shine our scales! Various types of livestock like the Bawng (12) and the georgious metallic blue glowing turkey-like birds. Huge oddly square and oblong-shaped vegetables like watermelon and gourds, and pots and pans to cook with made of silver and gold! Glasses to drink from made of an oddly purple-colored crystal!

Immediately I feel everyone starts to stare at us! They are pointing at us!

I noticed that all the dragon folk here are dressed in fine clothing!

Oops! We are NOT DRESSED!

One of the dragon folk quickly approaches us carrying two beautiful robes!

"You must not be new to our customs," she graciously replied.

"Yes! Thank you so much!" I quickly accept the garments and gave Bata (5) one, feeling very embarrassed!

"May I introduce myself and my companion. My name is Zennure (9). This is Bata (5), my young travel companion."

"What may I offer you for these fine robes?" Bata (5) remarks.

"Let me introduce myself, I am called the Caring One, Zaintzea (10). You may return the favor by telling all about my shop over here." Zaintzea (10) smiles.

Her shop was filled with delicious smelling meat and fruit pies, red, purple, and gold-colored fresh fruits! An assortment of georgious hand-sewn robes!

"Yes, we will be glad to!" I replied.

"Where do you recommend a place to go eat?"

"My life companion and our family have a café called Cibo Delizioso (11)!" Zaintzea (10) happily informs.

Leaving her assistant in charge of the store, Zaintzea (10) escorts us through the courtyard. The odd flowers and plants started barking and mooing at us! They mimic what they hear.

We walk through to a side street down to a georgious, illuminous white stucco and ruby red clay roof was the busy café, Cibo Delizioso (11).

There are eating areas outside designed for dragons. The seats were made of a green wood. It has shimmering crystals all through it. There are tables separate from each other, accompanied by a few chairs. The tops of the tables are made of pure silver! Most likely from the Gunong Perak (6).

The inside of the café was a cool temperature lit up brightly with Tuunich Ember (8) lamps. All the tables are full of dragon folk eating, except for one alongside the entry wall. Hanging on the walls are various types of vegetables and herbs ready to be cooked.

Bata (5) and I sit down. I'm getting worried, so I ask Zaintzea (10): "How can we pay for the meal? We have no currency," I inquired curiously.

Zaintzea (10) thinks for a moment.

"Would you be willing to help me out with a few chores around here?" she asks curiously.

"Will I be allowed to help too?" Bata (5) sheepishly inquired.

"Yes, of course, Bata (5)," Zaintzea (10) smiles.

"What would you like to eat?"

"I'm so hungry I could eat a herd of Bawng (12)!" Bata (5) answered jokingly.

"I don't think we have that here," Zaintzea (10) quietly laughed.

"How about some meat stew, Ragout de Viande (13)?" she asks.

"Yes, that would be great for both of us. Thank you!" I hungrily salivated.

Zennure In Dragon Form

Bata (5) In Dragon Form

# CHAPTER CUATRO (4)
# EXCITING ADVENTURES

We ate our delicious Ragout de Viande (13), which tasted like a venison stew. Then Zaintzea's (10) life companion, Fuerte (15), a very kind and muscular dragon, offered us shelter behind the Cibo Delizioso (11).

As Fuerte (15) escorts us to our white stucco cabin with a red roof, I see the orange neon fish "swimming" in a school, flying to their nightly shelter in the Yadi yadi (7) trees.

"Here we are." Fuerte (15) hands us the two beautifully handmade quilts he was carrying and a key.

"How long will you be staying? If you need me, Zaintzea (10) and I live above the Cibo Delizioso (11). There's stairs in the back to get to our door." Fuerte (15) smiles quietly, then retreats back to the café, Cibo Delizioso (11).

I paused for a moment.

"Bata (5), look at that Young Star setting in the southern sky! There's no moons up yet. It's glowing blue, red, and purple as it settles beneath the Silver Mountains, Gunong Perak (6)! It's so unbelievably gorgeous! I wonder what we will see tomorrow!"

***

The sounds of the morning woke me with a gentle nudge. There's a school of orange neon fish chirping in the nearest Crystal Bark trees: Arbore de Cortiza de Cristal (16). It sounds like a symphony of harps!

While stretching, I forget I have a long dragon tail. I accidentally knock over the purple water pitcher, and it spills on the floor! It falls with a crash!

While cleaning up the mess, Bata (5) appears in the doorway.

"What was that noise?" Bata (5) asks.

"Just stretching. Not to worry. Are you ready for breakfast?" I asked.

"I'm so hungry I could eat a neon fish!" he laughed. "How are we going to repay our kind hosts?" Bata (5) remarks thoughtfully.

"Let's go find out," I remark.

After faces are washed and fangs are cleaned, we happily march over to Cibo Delizioso (11) for our breakfast and awaited chores to repay our kind hosts.

After eating, Bata (5) and I gratefully take on our assignment of chores. When we finish, the Young Star is at the highest for the day: noon.

Bata (5) looks thoughtfully at the horizon.

"Zennure (9), I feel like an adventure! What can we do now?" he asks hopefully.

Just then I hear a crowd gathering in the street. The sound of Dwec (18) hooves clomping and screams after the cracking of a whip! The City Cryer is announcing something!

Bata (5) is startled.

"Zennure (9)! What's going on?"

"Hurry, we must go find out!" We rush to the city center.

"Hold up here! It might be trouble. I'll go ahead quietly and see, then I'll come get you," I tell Bata (5).

I creep slowly alongside the stucco buildings. The sounds of shouting and screams of pain grow increasingly louder! The City Cryer repeats:

"To all, to all, report to our Beloved Leader at the Castle of the Knowing One, Na Mananda (1), any knowledge of the new Strangers!"

As I run back to Bata (5), I hear scuffling and struggling!

"Let me go! I've done nothing wrong!"

It is Bata (5)! He's been captured! I rush to see what's going on. All of a sudden, I'm faced with none other than my old evil enemy!

"KYHA! (17)" I shout. "We mean no one harm! Bata (5) is with me!"

With an evil sneer, Kyha (17) recognizes me. His gravelly voice replies:

"I thought you were dead, Zennure (9)."

"So glad I could disappoint you, Kyha (17)," I say with a venomous laugh. "Let the young one go! We will report to the Castle of Na Mananda (1) without your help. We already had plans to go there today anyway." I scowl.

"So be it. But to make sure you get there, you will be put on the wagon!" Kyha (17) orders.

"You will put us nowhere!" I retort. "I will drive the wagon, and Bata (5) will sit beside me!"

"Very well. My Royal Mananda soldiers will accompany you." A dejected Kyha (17) shrugs.

I quickly scan the growing crowd of Dragon Folk. Amidst the onlookers stand an anxious Zaintzea (10) and Fuerte (15). I wave assuredly.

"We will return soon!"

At that, Bata (5) and I climb aboard the Royal Wagon. Taking control of the reins, I snap the orders:

"Dwec (18), onward!"

The blue-black Dwec (18), with the fiery blue glowing mane and tail, its long, pointed Mother of Pearl horn on its forehead shining like the rising moons, groan and begrudgingly pull against their harness. The Royal Wagon creaks and moans to a slow start.

Rising of the Young Star

# CHAPTER 5
# CINCO (19)
# SURPRISES AHEAD!

My mind races with every step of the Blue Black Dwec (18), and I wonder as the miles pass under the Royal Wagon. We've ascended and turned towards the east while the Royal Wagon creaks and sways, and the Royal Soldiers' armor clanks. In the late afternoon, the Young Star is growing ever dimmer through the shimmering clouds.

The well-travelled red, dusty road has taken us through the valley of Vita Rubia (3), now rising on a slope even higher through the Jade Arbores (7) forests.

On our right still is Gunong Perak (6), so I know we're still going south. The red dirt road has gradually changed to a rocky one. On our left, looking eastward behind us, is the Crystal Bark Forest. Beautifully twinkling, multicolored crystal rays of light shine through the green bark and the pearlite-yellow leaves.

I can hear the raging river passing under the Jade Tree and Crystal Green Bark construction bridge. I hear the clomping hooves of the Dwec (18) as they trot over the bridge.

Suddenly, a troop of armored bandits, Alaa Wutte Wutte (20), swoop up from underneath the bridge. Instinctively, I push Bata (5) underneath the wagon seat. The Royal Soldiers are armed with daggers and swords.

"Kyha (17)! Throw me a sword!" I demand. In a glinting flash, I catch a golden-handled sword, just in time. I feel a whoosh as a blade barely misses my arm.

Instantly, I am in war mode. I return the favor to my assailant, landing a slashing gash across his belly just under the armor. Before he can respond, I strike a knockout punch with my tail. Down he goes, into the rushing water of the river.

Sounds of gnashing teeth, clanks, thuds, and cries of pain follow the splashings of water. The Royal Soldiers and I quickly overcome the Tailless Lizards, Alaa Wutte Wutte (20).

A quick assessment of wounds, and we're back moving down the road.

"Why didn't we fly?" Bata (5) looks up at me innocently. "How far is it?"

"I suppose the Royal Soldiers' armor weighs them down," I guess.

We both laugh at the thought of the bullies struggling.

"Zennure (9), what's that on the horizon? I thought the Young Star was setting, but there are two glowing blue orbs in the sky!" Bata is startled.

"Oh my. The Two Moons, Uwer Uhar (21) of the Dusk. Rising in the south are two glowing blue orbs on each side of the Young Star, setting and aligned in a kaleidoscope like a red opal. Amazing oranges and reds burst with light. The two moons, indigo-blue, are glowing like phosphorus. The moons on each side of the Young Star create the most gorgeous light display one could imagine."

At last, the Dwec (18) enter through the castle gates. The drawbridge rises behind the Royal Wagon. I draw the reins to stop the Royal Wagon. There are a few Royal Soldiers guarding the gates. One of them approaches.

Kyha (17) calls one of the soldiers over.

"Go announce to the General that I have arrived with the strangers. They've come voluntarily," Kyha (17) orders. Turning to another Royal Soldier, he adds, "Show our guests where they can get something to eat while they wait for our Royal Leader."

"Zennure (9), you and Bata (5) may follow my second-in-command to our dinner quarters. There he will see to your needs," Kyha (17) announces.

I'm wondering why my nemesis, my lifetime enemy, is being unusually hospitable. What is he up to? And where are all The Knowing's beautiful animals? Even more so, where is our Creator, The Knowing, Na Mananda (1)?

# CHAPTER 6
# ANSWERS AT LAST!

Kyha's lieutenant led us through the dark dining room. I could just make out the long table for thirty men to eat. There were wooden chairs, simply made, and two metal chandeliers.

The lieutenant was carrying a strange type of candle. It was only a stick stuck through a metal tray with what looked like honey on it. There were hundreds of Lightning Bees swarming around it, lighting the way.

In the next room is the kitchen, a huge stone fireplace with copper pots and pans hanging around it. The fire is lit, warming the entire room. I welcomed the warmth. With the Young Star setting comes darkness, and even in the warm part of the year, it brings a freezing chill after dark.

He pointed to the table and chairs in the middle of the room.
"Make yourself comfortable," he gestured. "I will bring you something to eat."

While we sat at the castle kitchen table, I began to notice our surroundings. On each ironstone wall were Lightning Bee lamps with a mirror-polished silver plaque behind each one. The table where we sat was an old green wood worktable. The lieutenant had disappeared for a few minutes but reappeared with his arms laden with ingredients. He proceeded to prepare our meal, soup of some sort.

"What are you cooking?" Bata (5) asked. "What is your name?"

"I'm cooking Ragout de Viande (13), and my name is Lelle (22)," he replied.

The conversation was non-existent, but our meal was good. Still waiting to see Na Mananda (1), I impatiently asked,
"When are we going to see Na Mananda (1)? We've come a long way, and we're very anxious to see our Creator!"

"Then wait no more!" Kyha (17) announced. "Follow me."

Bata (5) and I followed my nemesis as requested. Down a long corridor, then to the left. All was dimly lit with Lightning Bee torches. The ironstone walls seemed to go on and on. At last, the Throne Room! The huge arched doors opened onto a bright and opulently red and gold decorated Throne Room. At the center of the room was the throne. But wait!

"You're not our Creator, Na Mananda (1)! Who are you?" I stated adamantly. "What have you done with our Creator?"

"You will show respect to our Leader!" Kyha (17) ordered.

"Leader?" I questioned. "Where is our Creator?"

Seated at the throne was the oldest dragon I could ever imagine. On its head were two rows of golden horns. Its skin hung off its bones and was covered in rough black and purple scales. Its eyes were red and yellow with the look of evil behind them.

"I am called Frare Mia Ancian (23). And who might you be?" it demanded. "I am the oldest brother of your beloved Creator," it growled. "Your Na Mananda (1) had to return to our homeland."

"I am called Zennure (9), and this is Bata (5)," I stated in disbelief. "When will Na Mananda (1) return? Why did she leave?"

"All will be answered in time, First One, Eerste Een (24)," Frare Mia Ancian (23) venomously spat.

"How did you know that?" I fought back the surprise in my voice. "No one calls me that except Na Mananda (1)!"

"You are boring me now. Go with Major Kyha (17) to your bed quarters," Frare Mia Ancian (23) sneered.

"Come with me," Kyha ordered.

We entered the doorway to the right of the undeserving host of the throne. Down a long, narrow staircase. The farther down we went, the colder it was, and the smell was increasingly pungent.

"What is that awful smell?" Bata (5) remarked. "Where are you taking us?"

"Stop right now!" I demanded. "We're not going any further! Come on, Bata, we're leaving!"

"Wait, please! You're our only hope!" Kyha (17) pleaded. "We're dying under Frare Mia Ancian's (23) rule!"

I stopped in my tracks. "Bata (5), wait a minute."

"What do you mean, Kyha (17)? What has really happened to Na Mananda (1)?" I urgently inquired.

"When Frare Mia Ancian (23) first arrived, Na Mananda (1) welcomed him happily. Frare Mia Ancian (23) was charming and kind to our Creator. She had no reason to doubt his words. After all, he was her brother. But Frare Mia Ancian (23) came with bad news," Kyha (17) continued. "He told Na Mananda (1) that their I Tinaq (25), Mother of Nature, was quickly fading into spirit form, her Spirit Breath, Souffle (26). She had to return to the land of her birth, Home Galaxy (30), Galeksi Rumah. Frare Mia Ancian (23) gained the trust of Na Mananda (1)."

"Na Mananda's home galaxy is born of the Spirit of the First Breath, now known as Spirit Breath, Souffle (26)," I told Bata (5). "That's the name of her home galaxy."

"Yes, she left Frare Mia Ancian in charge. He had decimated his own kingdom with heavy-handed, cruel overlord rule. His own kingdom, those that survived, rebelled against him and ran him out of his own realm. But Na Mananda (1) did not know that. I only found this out because I was posted to guard outside his quarters door. He talks about it in his sleep," Kyha (17) sounded desperate.

"Zennure (9), that horrible smell down here is all the animals and the Dragon Folk that Frare Mia Ancian (23) deemed either food for him, unnecessary, or rebellious against him. They are all in the dungeon starving! If he knew I was telling you about this, he would end my spirit!" Kyha (17) was adamant.

"Yes, Kyha, but what can be done? His Life Spirit, Eletzellem (27), is much stronger than mine," I asked.

"What did Frare Mia Ancian (23) mean when he called you Eerste Een (24)? Why didn't he destroy you for your impertinence?"

"I don't know if I should tell you about that," I answered cautiously.

"Know that I have wronged you in the past," Kyha (17) said. "But Na Mananda (1) taught me to be true to others as I would be to myself. I spent many years serving our Creator. I have become much stronger in my spirit."

"I understand," I replied. "Na Mananda (1) taught me to give a second chance to those who are willing to make it right. I will trust you to keep what I am about to tell you a secret to the end of your last breath," I cautioned.

"Are you sure you want to trust him, Zennure?" Bata (5) asked curiously.

"You have my word, Zennure (9). Now please tell me!" Kyha (17) pleaded.

"Yes, I promise I will not tell, Zennure (9)!" Bata (5) exclaimed.

"When Na Mananda (1) created our world, she also created me and my brothers and sisters. We have the strongest spirit, stronger than those she created after us," I explained.

"This means the First Born family have almost all the sight, intelligence, and creating abilities that Na Mananda (1) has. As long as we stay honest and true to our spirit, we will be strong in our abilities."

"Now that we know, where do we go from here?" Bata (5) remarked.

"I can use what we call Transporto Teleinine (28). This means that all the First Born family can transport ourselves and one other being through deep concentration of our minds," I explained. "I have to be in a safe, quiet place."

"What good does that do? We need to band together against Frare Mia Ancian (23)!" Kyha (17) pleaded.

"You will see very soon, Kyha. I will not tell you about it here for fear of you being tortured and infiltrated," I informed. "Now Bata (5) and I must leave."

Frare Mia Ancian

# CHAPTER 7
# COMING HOME!

Bata (5) and I step out of the castle into the cool night air. There were Tuunich Ember (8) torches lining all along the inside of the castle walls. This was causing a green glow reflection on mine and Bata's (5) scales, leaving a dream-like aura all around us.

"We must fly to the Opal Mountains to prepare for our Transporto Teleinine (28)."

"Is it very far?" Bata (5) worried.

"If you get tired, we will land and rest up," I reassured.

Off we flew towards the east, away from all that was familiar but towards security. We flew east alongside the Turquoise River, with the Ancient Hills on our right. I could smell the night air mixed with the scents of the singing Rabbit Flowers and see the wild Bawng (12) grazing as they moved along the river.

It had been a strenuous, long flight, but I could feel the sunrise beginning to break over the Northern Jade Arbores (7) and reaching over the Crystal Hills, which made a plethora of dazzling rainbows throughout the valley.

"At last, we're here! We will land over there beside that small cabin," I instructed.

"Is it safe?" Bata (5) worried.

"Yes, of course. This is where I used to live!" I assured. "Hopefully, there's no unwanted critters inside."

"Critters?!" Bata remarked astoundedly.

"We can still use Earthly words, can't we?" I laughed.

The cabin was nestled against a rocky hill covered by singing Rabbit Flowers. They're called that because instead of walking with their roots like other flowers, they hop!

The Rabbit Flowers absorbed the morning light and used it for energy. Their colors changed from a gorgeous metallic blue and then to red-orange-gold as they were fully charged.

There were Crystal Bark trees, Arbore de Cortiza (16), surrounding the front garden, giving rainbows to shade the cabin. When the breeze blew through the trees, it made wind chime–like twinkling sounds through the leaves.

The cabin was a bit abandoned-looking, but otherwise still intact, which surprised me, because I had left it in the care of my trusted friend, Cher Ami (29).

What has happened to her!? Perhaps she's been nesting her own eggs at her own home.

We landed in front of the cabin. I opened the green bark door, uncertain of what or who might be inside.

"Wait here, Bata (5). I have to be sure it's safe," I requested.

I entered the old green bark door and sniffed the air. I didn't smell anyone else in here.

The two arch-shaped windows on each side of the front door had orange Jade Tree, Jade Arbores de Cortiza (7), bark shutters. The shutters were closed, so I opened them and let in the morning light.

The front room was used for the kitchen and dining room. There were two sleeping chambers dug into the hill with secure bolting doors, so I entered and checked them thoroughly.

Standing in the front door, I called to Bata (5), who was dancing with a metallic orange-gold flower, dancing to the tune of the twinkling leaves of the Jade Trees, Arbore de Cortiza (7).

"Bata (5), come on in. It's safe now," I reported.

"Alright, Zennure (9)," he answered. Entering the cabin, he asked, "Why does the outside of the cabin match the background?"

"This cabin was built so I can retreat, rest, and possibly Transporto Teleinine (28). I have to have a safe, quiet place for that," I explained.

"Do you have anything to eat here? I'm really hungry and tired, Zennure (9)!" Bata (5) exclaimed.

"Yes, there's a garden. Maybe we'll find something out there. Let's go look."

It wasn't long before we had found, cooked, and eaten plenty of vegetables from my garden. We both were very tired and needed rest for our Transporto Teleinine (28) to see Na Mananda's home, Galeksi Rumah (30), when we wake.

# CHAPTER 8
# SETTING OUR SITES!

Bata (5) and I wake just before the setting of the Young Star. We eat and get ready for the Transporto Teleinine (28). I leave Cher Ami (29) a note, wishing her a fond farewell and thanking her for taking care of my property.

It is time now.

"Bata (5), let's sit here in the dining room chairs. We need to close our eyes and concentrate. Think about the same thing!" I instructed.

"Now think Na Mananda, Na Mananda, Na Mananda (1)."

I see in my mind an electric blue glowing, swirling light beginning to pull us through time and space. We see each other as we pass through all the galaxies made by Na Mananda (1).

Suddenly all is black. Now there's a small glowing green swirl before us. It's constantly growing brighter as well as pulling us through it. We see oddly shaped planets like triangles, squares, and oblongs. Stars are brightly neon multicolors and shaped like spirals spinning lengthwise.

Na Mananda's Life Spirit, Eletzellem (27), is close by. I can feel it. The glowing green swirl turns into a still, quiet neon blue tunnel with a small pulsing white light at the end. Gently pulling us through the tunnel, the white light grows bigger.

At last, we have landed on Souffle (26), Na Mananda's Mother of Nature, I Tinaq (25), home world.

This world is so different. There are trees, but they're all different: triangular, round, and oblong. The light of the planet is neon glowing blue. It's like we're underwater. When we step, the ground beneath our feet glows neon green. It seems that the grass reacts to the touch of our feet.

I see hills shaped like pencils stacked sideways together, with orange, red, and purple coral growing all over them.

The air is thick when we try to walk through it, like water. But it's air, because we can breathe.

"Bata, do you know how to swim?" I asked.

"Yes, Zennure (9). Can't we fly in this world?" Bata (5) remarked.

"Let's just try to swim as we walk," I replied. "We need to find Na Mananda (1). Let's sit under this embankment of purple coral. I'm going to try to echolocate her."

"You mean like a dolphin?" Bata (5) asked curiously.

"Yes, Bata. Like a dolphin," I answered. "Now both of us need to say over and over, Na Mananda. Na Mananda."

We sat chanting our Creator's name until I got a nudge on my nose. I opened my eyes.

"Na Mananda! You're here!" I exclaimed. "I'm so glad to see you! This is Bata (5)!"

Na Mananda was as glorious as ever. She was in her Dragon form, her glowing white-green opal scales and her blue opalescent eyes. She smiled down upon us.

"Thee hath travelled a long way to see me! What doth thine journey entail?" she enquired.

Bata (5), being a child, whispered to me, "What did she say?"

"She asked, why are we here?" I explained.

"My dearest Na Mananda! It's so wonderful to see you at last! How is your Mother of Nature, I Tinaq (25)? I was told by Kyha (17) that you were tricked into coming here.

But I must be the bearer of bad news. Your oldest brother, Frare Mia Ancian (23), told you that I Tinaq (25) was very ill. He has taken over Mundu Ederra (2). He is more evil than we ever imagined. He has killed all the Dragon Folk who dared to oppose him, jailed all who can't pay his outrageous taxes, and all the animals that he chooses to eat he cages them in the dungeon. Please return with us!" I pleaded.

"My dearest Eerste Een (24)! Your journey is not in vain. I have seen my Mother of Nature, I Tinaq (25). She is very well. She is also very wise. She told me that you were coming and why. My brother's evil has made him weak in his Life Spirit, Eletzellem (27). We will now return in my own Transporto Teleinine (28).

Both of you, hold my claw! Think of where we need to go, to my castle! Now we'll concentrate! Hold on!" Na Mananda (1) instructed.

# CHAPTER 9
# RETURN TO MUNDU EDERRA

We're holding onto Na Mananda's (1) claw, with our eyes open, and an opalescent arch appears before us! We step through the swirling rainbow light, and all of a sudden, we're back in Mundu Ederra (2)!

"Wow! That was fast!" Bata (5) remarked astoundedly.

In the dark courtyard, there were metallic orange flames dancing from the metal torches all along the inside of the castle walls and in the doorway. There were Royal Soldiers guarding the doorway of the castle.

"We're back in the courtyard of your beloved castle, aren't we?" I asked.

"Yes, Eerste Een (24), you must promise you will step aside and let me deal with my brother," Na Mananda (1) answered.

"If you insist, my Beloved Creator," I replied, still holding Bata's (5) claw.

Suddenly, in the middle of the courtyard, a black opal vortex opened! Frare Mia Ancian (23) stepped through with a thud.

"So, you've returned, Na Mananda (1)! I suppose you want me gone from this land!" Frare Mia Ancian (23) venomously spewed.

"You have broken the Laws of I Tinaq (25)! For that, you cannot be forgiven!" Na Mananda (1) ruled.

"You are much younger than me, Na Mananda (1), therefore much weaker!" Frare Mia Ancian (23) hatefully laughed. "You are no match to my Life Spirit (27)! I am claiming your kingdom, and you can do nothing about it!"

Just then, Frare Mia Ancian (23) burst out a painfully loud roar, followed by a blast of blue glowing flames dancing around Na Mananda's (1) feet.

"Challenge accepted, Frare Mia Ancian (23)!" Na Mananda (1), unfurling her wings, took flight as she bloomed green, yellow, and white flames straight at Frare Mia Ancian (23), knocking him down with a powerful blast.

Her evil brother groaned in pain. Picking himself up, he shook off the aches. Taking to flight himself, he inhaled deeply in preparation for another blast of fire.

Before he could release his fire, Na Mananda (1) bellowed a deafening screech mixed with a Mundu Ederra (2)–quaking blast of neon blue, orange, and white ice fire.

The evil brother was instantly engulfed in burning ice. Unable to move nor fly, Na Mananda's (1) evil brother fell to the ground, shattering into a thousand evil pieces.

Na Mananda (1) landed in the Royal Courtyard as she watched her evil brother's Eletzellem (27) vanish in a red, green, and blue puff of smoke. At last, Frare Mia Ancian's (23) evil rule was Over!

# CHAPTER 10
# MISSION ACCOMPLISHED!

Word quickly spread of Na Mananda's (1) triumphant return! All the Dragon Folk gathered at the Royal Courtyard.

There was music, dancing, and rows upon rows of tables with roasted Bawng (12), delicious Ragout de Viande (13), and strangely shaped fruits and vegetables.

At last, I could see all of my family and friends!

"Now this is what I call a celebration!" Bata (5) breathed a sigh of relief.

Even though we must return to our Earthly time and space, we will return next time with Your Brother, My Son!

ENDING IS ONLY TEMPORARY
CHER AMI (29)